Dedicated to all
Police Officers
and their families.

Be safe always.

The **ACADEMY** is where recruits train to learn the skills they need to become police officers!

Police officers wear a **BADGE** to identify themselves and represent who they work for.

Police officers drive specially marked **CARS** with flashing lights and sirens!

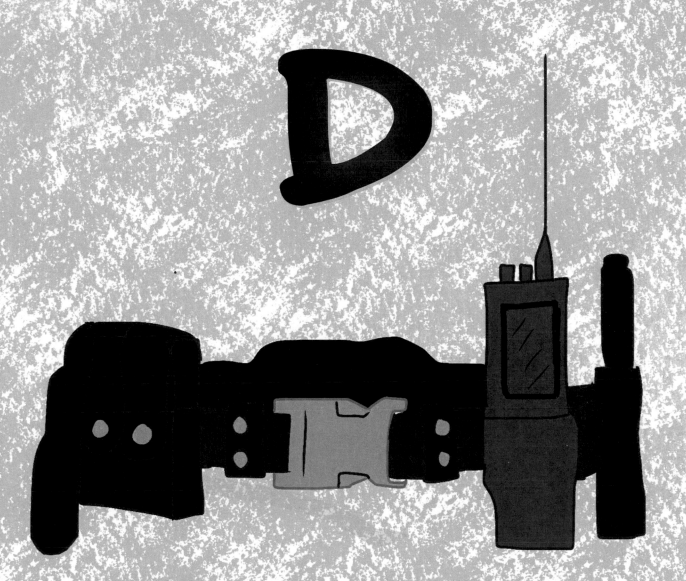

D

A **DUTY BELT** is used to hold all the tools Police Officers need to use while working.

E

EVIDENCE is used to help solve crimes!

When Police Officers work at night or in dark places they use their FLASHLIGHT to see all around.

Police
Officers
carry a
GUN
and are
trained
how to
use it
safely.

G

Police Officers put
HANDCUFFS on a person
when they are arrested.

An **INVESTIGATION** takes place to figure out what happened at a crime scene or to solve a mystery.

Criminals are taken to JAIL when they disobey the law.

Some Police Officers work the
MIDNIGHT SHIFT
and they work all through the night
when most people are asleep!

Name Tag

N

Police Officers wear a **NAME TAG** as part of their uniform to identify themselves.

A **POLICE STATION** is where Police Officers report for work.

Police officers must be
QUICK, especially if they
have to chase a criminal!

R

Police officers use a **RADIO** to relay messages back and forth to one another or to call for back up.

Each road has a
SPEED LIMIT
that people must follow, and
Police Officers make sure
nobody is going too fast!

U

Police **UNIFORMS** vary from department to department.

Police Officers wear a **VEST** to

help keep them protected and safe.

If you see a School **X-ING** area, you may see a Police Officer helping kids get across the street to school safely!

A **_YIELD SIGN_** is another road sign that people follow to drive safely.

Some areas, like School **ZONES** have slower speed limits and more Police patrolling to keep kids safe!

Made in the USA
Las Vegas, NV
12 October 2022